11/92   1/1

For Margery,
a master at ground control and lover of lift-off

Library of Congress Cataloging-in-Publication Data
Woodruff, Elvira.
The wing shop / written by Elvira Woodruff :
illustrated by Stephen Gammell.   1st ed.
p. cm.
Summary: After his family moves to a different part of town,
Matthew tries to get back to his old house by trying on
different pairs of wings in an unusual wing shop.
ISBN 0-8234-0825-6
[1. Flight—Fiction.   2. Moving, Household—Fiction.]
I. Gammell, Stephen, ill. II. Title.
PZ7.W8606Wi   1990
[E]   dc20   90-55094   CIP   AC
ISBN 0-8234-0825-6

The Wing Shop

by ELVIRA WOODRUFF

illustrated by STEPHEN GAMMELL

Holiday House / New York

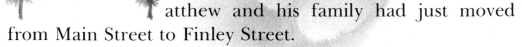

atthew and his family had just moved from Main Street to Finley Street.

"I don't like it on Finley Street," thought Matthew. "It's too far from my old neighborhood. And nothing is the same." The house was different. "Too new looking," he thought. And the kids were different. "Too big looking," he thought. Even the porch steps weren't right. "Too skinny," he thought.

When Matthew asked his mother if they could move back, she just smiled and said, "This is our home now, you'll get used to it."

"Never," he thought.

Matthew began to wonder just how he could get back to Main Street. He was too young to drive a car. He was too little to take the bus alone, and his mother said he was not to walk past the drugstore.

One day, while Matthew was playing outside, he began to follow a pigeon.

"If I had wings, I could fly back to Main Street," he thought. "But where can I get wings?" he wondered.

Suddenly Matthew stopped. The pigeon had flown up to a pair of wooden wings hanging over the door of a dusty old shop.

"Wings are just what I need," thought Matthew, as he opened the door. Once inside he stopped and stared. It was unlike any store he had ever seen. Swirling and flapping wings of every size, shape, and color hung from the wooden shelves.

A very thin little girl with red fuzzy hair stood on a stool dusting a pair of chicken wings.

"Hello," said the girl. "My name is Lucy Featherman, may I help you?"

"Yes," replied Matthew, "I need a pair of wings."

"We've got plenty of those," Lucy said. "What kind do you need?"

"Well, I don't know," said Matthew. "Do you have a pair that can get me back to Main Street?"

The girl frowned and looked around the store. "I really don't know," she explained. "You see, I'm just watching the store for my grandfather. He went out to test some firefly wings last night and hasn't come back yet. Why don't you try on a pair?"

Matthew decided on a pair of lovely gray and white ones.

"Oh, you look wonderful," Lucy told him. "But don't you want to take off your socks and shoes?"

Just as Matthew bent down to untie his sneakers, a great gust of wind from an open window picked him up, and his wings began to flap! Before he knew it, he was flying out of the shop!

"Oh well, that's a good idea," said Lucy. "Go for a test flight and see if you like them. Don't worry, they're guaranteed to bring you back."

But Matthew *was* worried! He had never flown before, and it felt very strange to be so far off the ground! He was flying high above the city's buildings. "This doesn't seem like the way back to Main Street," Matthew thought as he headed out to the harbor.

When he reached the ocean, the wings began to glide in close to the water. Matthew was having fun until the wings swooped down as if they were looking for fish.

Matthew's sneakers got soggy, his hair got wet, and he kept getting salt water up his nose! "I'll never get to Main Street this way," he thought. "I wish these wings would take me back to the store."

No sooner had he said that than the wings lifted him from the water and flew him to Finley Street. He sailed through the large window of Featherman's Wing Shop.

"Oh, I'm so sorry," Lucy apologized, as she helped Matthew dry off. "I guess sea gull wings aren't really what you're looking for. I wish Grandpa were here to help."

As Lucy put the towel down, her hand rested on a shelf filled with leathery, black wings. "These might be just the thing," she said.

"I'm feeling kind of seasick. Are you sure they're not sea gull wings?" Matthew asked as he tried them on.

"There isn't any tag, but I can look them up in Grandpa's inventory book, so we can tell just what kind they are," Lucy told him.

But before she could open the large book, Matthew began to fly around the room. "I guess you'll have to give them a try," Lucy called as Matthew flew up and out the window!

This time the leathery black wings carried him far away from the city. Instead of flying to the ocean, Matthew was flying over fields and barns. He was in the country. He had never seen a real cow or pig before. "Moo, moo, oinky, oink," he called down to the farm animals. But just as he was enjoying himself, the black wings swooped him through the window of an old barn.

Matthew found himself in the loft. It was hot and stuffy, and the wings had turned him upside down! "What kind of crazy wings are these?" Matthew wondered, as he swung from the rafters. "I wish they would take me back to the store."

Just as he wished, the wings turned him right side up and flew him all the way to Finley Street. Matthew sailed through the big window and landed on the counter.

"I guess you didn't make it to Main Street," Lucy said in a rather small voice. BAT WINGS she wrote on a sticker and stuck it to the wings as Matthew took them off.

"I do wish Grandpa would mark these things," she said with a sigh.

As Matthew sat down to rest, he noticed a small pair of gleaming airplane wings sitting on a display case. "If these were bigger, I bet they could get me back to Main Street," he said.

Lucy helped pin them on. "Don't worry, the tag says expansible," she told him. No sooner had she pinned them on than they began to grow, and Matthew found himself zooming out the window! By the time he was above the street, the airplane wings had grown to full size. They were so big that they couldn't fit between the buildings. Matthew began to circle over the roofs.

"Stop," Matthew called to the wings. "There it is! There's Main Street!" But the airplane wings were much too big to land.

Matthew looked down at his old street and frowned. His house was where it always had been, but its big beautiful white porch was now painted a horrible pink. Even the steps were pink, except now instead of Matthew and his brother playing on them, three new children were there!

"Yuck," Matthew yelled. "What have you done to my house?"

"This is *our* house now. We live here, not you. Go away," they yelled back.

Before he knew it, Matthew was gliding over more houses and buildings. Suddenly he saw something below. "Hey, look down there," he called to the wings. "It's Finley Street! Hi, everybody," he shouted. He could see his whole family below him. His mother was hanging out clothes, his father was sitting on the porch reading the paper, and his little brother was playing on the steps.

Seeing them all together like that made Matthew smile. It almost made Finley Street look a little like his old home before all the pink. "Supper is ready," Matthew's mother called. Matthew realized how hungry all this flying had made him. He closed his eyes and wished himself back to the wing shop.

Suddenly the wings began to shrink, and before Matthew knew it, he was gliding through the big window of Featherman's Shop. He landed on the top shelf. Lucy had to help him down with a ladder.

"Did you get back to Main Street?" she asked.

"No, these wings are too big," Matthew said.

"Oh, I should have thought of that," said Lucy.

"Well, how about these? They're imported butterfly wings. You can get back to Main Street in style with these."

"Thanks," said Matthew. "But it's my suppertime now. And I don't think I can live on Main Street anymore. There are new kids living there, and my old house is not the same."

"Oh, I'm sorry." Lucy frowned. "But you know, I'd forgotten that we were having a sale on bee wings today. Since you've been such a good customer, why don't you use these to get home, no charge." She smiled as she lifted a tiny velvet tray from the shelf.

"Are you sure they'll take me home? Home to Finley Street?" Matthew looked wary as Lucy pinned the delicate little wings to the back of his sweatshirt.

Suddenly there was a great flurry of buzzing, as Matthew was lifted off the floor and out the shop's window! He hadn't gotten far when he zoomed down and hung dangling over the window box in front of the bakery. His face was in a geranium!

"Good-bye," called Lucy from the window. "And remember, Grandfather is getting in new shipments all the time, so try and come again. Oh, and don't worry, you'll get home."